Parents and Caregivers,

Stone Arch Readers are designed to provide enjoyable reading experiences, as well as opportunities to develop vocabulary, literacy skills, and comprehension. Here are a few ways to support your beginning reader:

- Talk with your child about the ideas addressed in the story.

- Discuss each illustration, mentioning the characters, where they are, and what they are doing.

- Read with expression, pointing to each word. You may want to read the whole story through and then revisit parts of the story to ensure that the meanings of words or phrases are understood.

- Talk about why the character did what he or she did and what your child would do in that situation.

- Help your child connect with characters and events in the story.

Remember, reading with your child should be fun, not forced. Each moment spent reading with your child is a priceless investment in his or her literacy life.

Gail Saunders-Smith, Ph.D.

STONE ARCH READERS

are published by Stone Arch Books
A Capstone Imprint
1710 Roe Crest Drive
North Mankato, Minnesota 56003
www.capstonepub.com

Library of Congress Cataloging-in-Publication Data
    Meister, Cari.
    The stranded orca / by Cari Meister; illustrated by Steve Harpster.
    p. cm. — (Stone Arch readers—ocean tales)
    Summary: Bruno the orca is stranded on the beach--can his friends come up
with a plan to rescue him in time?
    ISBN 978-1-4342-4026-2 (library binding) — ISBN 978-1-4342-4232-7 (pbk.)
    1. Killer whale—Juvenile fiction. 2. Friendship—Juvenile fiction. 3. Rescues—
Juvenile fiction. [1. Killer whale—Fiction. 2. Whales—Fiction. 3. Friendship—
Fiction. 4. Rescues—Fiction.] I. Harpster, Steve, ill. II. Title.
PZ7.M515916.Str 2012
[E]—dc23

                        2011050083

                    Art Director: Kay Fraser
                    Designer: Russell Griesmer
                Production Specialist: Kathy McColley

                    Reading Consultants:

                Gail Saunders-Smith, Ph.D.
                Melinda Melton Crow, M.Ed.
            Laurie K. Holland, Media Specialist

                    Printed in China
        032012   006677RRDF12

The Stranded ORCA

by Cari Meister

illustrated by Steve Harpster

STONE ARCH BOOKS
a capstone imprint

BRUNO THE ORCA

ORCA FUN FACTS

- An orca is about the same size as a bus, and it weighs about six tons.

- An average-size orca eats about 500 pounds of food a day.

- The fin on the back of a male orca can stand up to six feet tall.

- Orcas use clicks and whistles to talk to each other. Each group of orcas have their own unique language.

Bruno was the biggest whale
in the orca pod.

He was strong and fast, too.
Once his friend Peeper clocked
him swimming thirty miles per
hour!

Bruno's teeth were long,
white, and very sharp. Brave
and fierce, he was the best
hunter in the pod.

Bruno always shared his food.

"Thanks, Bruno!" said Duke and Peeper.

"My pleasure," said Bruno.

One day when Bruno was hunting seals, he got stranded on the beach. His speed and sharp teeth could not help him.

"What am I going to do?" he asked sadly.

"Oh, no!" said Peeper. "Bruno is stuck."

"He will die if he doesn't get back in the water," said Duke.

"We must help him!" said Peeper. "But how?"

Peeper squealed to Bruno. "Hang in there, Bruno," she said. "We will help you."

Bruno squealed back. He
knew he didn't have much
time. His skin was drying out.

Peeper and Duke raced along the coast.

"We need a plan, but what?" asked Duke.

Then Peeper saw something
in the distance.

"I know where we can get
help," she said. "Follow me!"

"A sight-seeing boat!" shouted Duke.

"Humans love our tricks," said Peeper. "If they see us, they might follow us to Bruno. Then they can help him."

Duke and Peeper put on the best show for the boat.

They jumped.

They flipped.

They slapped their flippers.

The humans loved the orca
show! They took pictures. They
clapped and cheered.

"I think they will follow us,"
said Peeper.

Peeper and Duke led the way
to Bruno.

Look," said the captain, "a stranded whale! I'll call for help."

Soon, people arrived in rescue boats. They put large, wet tarps over Bruno.

"The humans are trying to keep him wet," said Duke.

Peeper and Duke squealed out to Bruno.

He squealed back. "I think I am going to make it!" he said.

The humans worked very hard. Bruno clicked to tell them thank you. Soon, a large boat with a crane lifted Bruno.

"What are they doing?" asked
Peeper.

"I think they are bringing him
out to deeper water," said Duke.

Duke was right. Soon Bruno was free!

"Thank you!" he squealed to the humans.

Bruno jumped and slapped his tail.

"Thank you!" he said to Peeper and Duke. "Thank you for helping me!"

The End

STORY WORDS

orca	squealed
fierce	distance
pleasure	rescue
stranded	humans

Total Word Count: 381

WHO ELSE IS SWIMMING IN THE OCEAN?